Queen is Quiet

and other ABC Tongue Twisters

Erika Barriga

Aa

Apple flies through the
air in an airplane.

Bb

Bear wears boots
and has a belly button.

Cc

Cat craves a slice of chocolate cake.

Dd

Duck will take a dip
with a donut.

Ee

Elephant has ears
and wears earmuffs.

Ff

Fox eats his food
with forks.

Gg

Giant bunny wears
gloves and gives gifts.

Hh

House wears a hat while
hearts hover high.

Ii

Iguana eats ice cream.

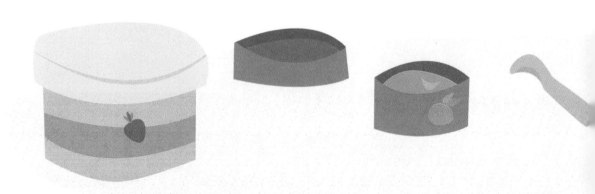

Jj

Jester juggles jellybeans.

Kk

Koala cuddles his
kosher ketchup.

Ll

Lemon licks the lollipop.

Mm

Monkey drinks milk
and eats mangos.

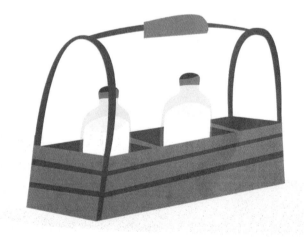

Nn

Nerdy nectarine is nice.

Otter has one tooth
and wears orange socks.

Pp

Pigs and plants are
a perfect pair.

Qq

Queen quail is quiet.

ssssshhhhhhhhhhhhhhh......

Rr

beep, beep, bop boop!

Robot radish loves rainbows.

Ss

Squirrel skates and
wants to share
a sandwich.

Tt

The land of tiny trees
and tulips.

Uu

Unicorn is under umbrellas.

Vases have very
small voices.

Watermelon wears a
watch on his wrist.

Xylophone is extra
excited!

Yy

Yam will yak about his yellow yo-yo.

yakkity yak yak yak!

Zz

Zen zucchini is in the zone.

About the Author

Erika Barriga is an author/illustrator working in Denver, CO. She loves creating in digital media as well as watercolor. She thinks there is nothing better than getting immersed in a good book and hopes to help kids do the same. When she isn't painting or drawing you can find her playing with her baby girl or capturing moments with photography.

Print ISBN: 9781623954901
eISBN: 9781623954932
ePub ISBN: 9781623954949
Published in the United States by Xist Publishing
www.xistpublishing.com
PO Box 61593 Irvine, CA 92602

First Edition